Papa Alonzo Leatherby

Simon & Schuster Books for Young Readers

Papa Alonzo Leatherby

A Collection of Tall Tales from
the Best Storyteller in Carroll County

by Marguerite W. Davol

SIMON & SCHUSTER BOOKS FOR YOUNG READERS
An imprint of Simon & Schuster Children's Publishing Division
1230 Avenue of the Americas
New York, New York 10020
Text copyright © 1995 by Marguerite W. Davol
Frontispiece © 1995 by Rebecca Leer

Simon & Schuster Books for Young Readers is a trademark of
Simon & Schuster
Designed by Virginia Pope
The text of this book is set in 13-point Cochin
Manufactured in the United States of America

10 9 8 7 6 5 4 3 2 1

Library of Congress Cataloging-in-Publication Data
Davol, Marguerite W.
Papa Alonzo Leatherby: A Collection of Tall Tales from the best
storyteller in Carroll County / by Marguerite W. Davol; illustrated by
Rebecca Leer.
p.   cm.
Summary: When Papa Alonzo Leatherby's tall tales about New England
freeze solid one extra cold winter, they have to be thawed out and pre-
served in ingenious ways.
[1. Tall tales. 2. New England-Fiction.] I. Leer, Rebecca, ill. II. Title.
PZ7.D32155Pap 1995
[Fic]-dc20   94-19372
                                                          CIP
                                                          AC
ISBN: 0-689-80278-1

Contents

For Hannah and Jesse, who love books and blueberries.
-M.D.

I.

The Coldest Night of the Year

P apa Alonzo Leatherby lived a long, long time ago. He lived *so* long ago that nobody in Carroll County had even heard of automobiles, much less seen one. Nor airplanes. If people wanted to get from one place to another, they rode a horse. Or else walked. Mostly, people walked.

Of course, way back then, there weren't radios, either, leastways, not in the little house in the woods where Papa Alonzo and the Leatherby family lived. As for television, why nobody'd thought it up yet!

What did Papa Alonzo and his wife, Lulie, and their nine children do for entertainment? Well, Saturday night they might hitch up their horse, Macduff, pile into the wagon, and drive over to Tamworth Grange Hall for a sing-along or square dance. But most of the time, they listened to Papa Alonzo tell stories—all about when he was young, all about farm and forest—stories for every season of the year. Papa Alonzo told stories to anyone who'd listen, and after awhile he became known as the best story-

teller in Carroll County. A champion storyteller, that's
what he was.

The Leatherby children—five girls and four boys
—loved to hear their father's tales. When something
reminded Papa Alonzo of a story, he'd clear his throat
and say, "Well, now, as I recollect…" which was the
way he always began. Hearing those words, Lulie and
the children would gather around, waiting. And then
Papa Alonzo would commence to tell his tale about
the day the goat turned blue. Or how his dog got its
name. But one year, believe it or not, Papa Alonzo
didn't tell any stories to his family, not a one….

E arly one winter morning, it started to snow. It
snowed and snowed. And the snowflakes
that fell were huge. Humongous! Giant-
gigantic! Why, they were so large that when one of
them fell on Papa's dog, Willy, it knocked him flatter
than a pancake. If Papa Alonzo hadn't been right
there to scoop Willy up and sort of push him and pull
him and pummel him back into shape, that dog probably would have spent the rest of his days as a fur rug
on the parlor floor. Quick as a weasel's wink, Papa
Alonzo grabbed up Willy and hurried the both of
them into the house. Besides worrying about Willy,
Papa had a headache from all those huge snowflakes
thunking him on the head.

By the time breakfast was over, snow covered the
front steps right up to the bottom of the door. But it

didn't quit. By lunch time, the snow was as high as the window sills. But it didn't quit. And by the time supper was on the table, snow had piled higher than the window tops and covered all the doors. But still it didn't quit. Those enormous snowflakes kept dropping down from the sky and drifting up against Papa Alonzo's little house in the woods. The snow didn't stop until the house was buried right up to its roof. It was a mighty good thing that the snow quit then or one of those gigantic flakes might have slid down the chimney and put the fire out!

The snow stopped, but then a frigid wind straight out of the North Pole began to howl round the chimney, threatening to suck the fire right up out of the fireplace. And that night turned out to be the coldest night anybody ever remembered. It got so cold that even sitting close to the fireplace, the whole family had to wrap themselves in shawls and blankets to keep warm.

In fact, it was so cold that when Papa Alonzo began to tell a story—"Ahem. Well, now, as I recollect..."—something odd happened. *His words froze.* Yep, all those words turned into solid ice, right there in midair. Not a sound except for the north wind screeching around the chimney. Lulie and the nine Leatherbys, from thirteen-year-old Martha to baby Moses, didn't hear a single word that Papa Alonzo was saying, because every last syllable was frozen solid. But they could see all his words just hanging there in the air.

Now Lulie was as sharp as an icicle and as quick as an avalanche. She jumped up and grabbed a bunch of those frozen words, plucked them right out of the air, and threw them into the big kettle of soup simmering on the iron cook stove. The words began to melt, little by little, and pretty soon, everybody could hear, "Well, now, as I recollect..." and one of Papa Alonzo's tales would begin. And that's how the family spent the night, listening to one after another of Papa Alonzo's melted stories. Of course, once in a while one of his words would be a little hard to understand—all tangled up as it was with a slice of onion or a chunk of celery in that soup kettle. But the stories kept on until everyone fell asleep.

Nobody knew exactly when morning came. It was impossible to tell when the sun rose and when the sun set with snow covering all the windows and doors. So the whole family ate soup and slept and in between times huddled around the fireplace. There they'd watch each of Papa Alonzo's stories freeze in midair. Then, once the words thawed out on the stove, everybody would settle back and listen.

Finally, by evening of the next day, the wind shifted to the south; and it warmed up enough so the family could begin to dig itself out. A good thing, too. After all those hours of recollecting, Papa Alonzo had just about run out of stories to tell.

In fact, he did not tell one more story for the rest of that year. He didn't need to. Because, as it turned out, Lulie missed a lot of those frozen words. She'd grabbed fast because all that ice was so cold, and a lot of the words slipped right out of her hands. They never got to the soup kettle to thaw. Instead, words from all those tales dropped into the nooks and crannies of the little house. The rest of that winter, whenever Lulie baked bread or muffins and the oven warmed up the house more than usual, some of the frozen words would thaw and another of Papa Alonzo's tales could be heard. Now sometimes the words didn't make sense, all jumbled together any which way. Then Lulie'd have to use her egg beater and whisk them into shape!

If nobody was around to listen, Lulie would pick up the words and set to work canning the tales so's they wouldn't spoil. And she felt mighty proud of her neatly labeled glass jars lined up all in a row on the pantry shelf, ready to open when the right season arrived.

Along about the middle of March, the very last of all those words melted. Actually, they weren't really words at all but Papa Alonzo's loud snores, which had frozen while everyone slept that coldest winter night. And Lulie, who always hated to waste anything, just stuffed those snores into the pickle barrel and clapped the lid on tight. One hot July night, the twins were hungry for pickles. Lifting the barrel lid, they let loose some of Papa Alonzo's vinegary snores. Papa Alonzo nearly jumped out of his suspenders. He'd never heard himself snore before! Besides, Lulie discovered that pickled snores were great for scaring mosquitoes away!

People might wonder about whether all of this really happened. Well, Papa Alonzo has told everybody the story himself, so it must be true. After all, he's the champion storyteller of Carroll County. And if anyone wants to hear one of his tales, all they need to do is to take down one of Lulie's jars from the pantry shelf and open the lid. And listen.

II.

The Mammoth Maple

N ine Leatherbys—a heap of younguns and each one as different as snowflake patterns. Martha, the oldest, was born talking and hadn't stopped since! That girl could talk worms out of apples and bark off a tree. Why, she could talk ears off a corn stalk and honey out of a beehive. Whenever blustery March winds rattled the windows, the Leatherbys teased with "Windy Martha's jabbering again!" She'd just laugh and say, "I love to talk!"

The one thing Martha didn't talk about was her secret ambition. More than anything in the world, she wanted to become a champion storyteller like Papa Alonzo.

One March morning, Papa Alonzo was out in the barn, carving a plug for a leaky syrup barrel. He'd discovered that syrup had seeped onto the barn floor, making it so sticky the cows couldn't moo or move, and the milk pails stuck where they stood. In fact, Papa Alonzo had to strap on his skis, slipperied with goose grease, so he wouldn't stick to the floor, himself!

In the kitchen, however, nine younguns gobbled up pancakes smothered with maple syrup. Busy chattering, Martha tipped the syrup jug up, up, upside down. "Empty!" she complained. "There's never enough syrup to go around."

She headed for the pantry, still talking, and returned with a heavy jar. But when she opened it to refill the jug, instead of syrup, words spilled out.

"Ah! That's one of Papa Alonzo's stories I canned," Lulie said. "Stop gibble-gabbling, Martha! Let's listen to the maple tree tale."

Martha stuffed her mouth full of pancakes and listened.

W ell, now, as I recollect...maple syrup on snow was a favorite treat all my sprouting-up years, but not for the past two years. Nope, not since the spring of '99. That whole year was unusual, all right, if you younguns remember, with everything growing sort of peculiar-like. One week a January thaw was so warm that dandelions poked green out of the ground and maple buds bulged; the next week was so cold that Macduff's hooves froze tight to the ground. Yep, I had to get my ax and chop that horse free so we could ride over to Conway for Maddy Bickford's wedding.

With such cold, all the wild animals suffered, even the snowshoe rabbits, believe it or not. Couldn't see them waiting outside, of course, all white against the snow, but every time we'd open the door, there'd be a whoosh of white across our boots. A pair of rabbits would dash in, lickety-larrup, and crouch close to the stove, shivering from the tips of their flop ears to the tufts of their tails.

Why, come night there'd hardly be room enough in the bed to sleep, for all the cold-nosed rabbits snuggling down under the quilts to keep warm. We didn't have the heart to turn the poor critters away, did we? In fact, those snowshoe rabbits were mighty grateful we'd kept them from freezing. When they molted that year and their fur changed from white to brown, the long-eared beasties gathered up all their leftover fur and wove it into a white comforter for Lulie and me. To this very day, it keeps us toasty-warm all winter.

Of course, spring returned, as always, and the rabbits hopped away. Come March when days turned sunny and warm but nights were still frost-cold, I knew it was time to think about maple syrup — time to head for the deep woods, find me some big sugar maples, and tap them.

So one bright day I hitched Macduff to the sledge, gathered up all the sap buckets and the new spouts I'd whittled on winter nights, and set out. Willy hopped onto the sledge at the last minute — that dog always hates to be left behind!

Melting snow made bottomless mud puddles of the roads, but in the deep woods where I headed, snow lay thick among the trees. The horse had tough sledding and I had to keep yelling, "Lay on, Macduff! Lay on."

Busy trying to maneuver the horse and that big sledge through deep drifts and around boulders and trees, I wasn't much watching where I was going. Now I wasn't exactly lost, you understand, but…. When I finally stopped for a breather, I found myself in a part of the forest I'd never seen before. All of a sudden, sping-spang in front of me was the most enormous sugar maple I'd ever laid eyes on! Why, that tree was so huge that you could have started walking around it at noon and not met yourself coming or going until dark. And tall! Its bare branches stretched so high that its top plain disappeared into the clouds.

A perfect tree to tap, I thought, so I went to work. I chose a sturdy birchwood spout and began to bore a hole in the tree trunk. I'd barely pushed in the spout, and before I could hang a bucket on it—whoosh! I had to leap back out of the way! The sap from that tree came out so thick and so fast it almost knocked me off my feet. Well, I quick grabbed a bucket and before I could sing out "ninety-nine buckets of sap to boil," the thing was brim-filled. I grabbed a second bucket, and then another and another, each one filling up faster than an owl can flick its eye. Had to be mighty careful, too. That stream of sap threatened to carry me off, it was so powerful.

I needed help! But I couldn't just leave all that sap spurting out onto the ground. Why, it would have drowned poor Macduff, the sledge, and me, too, the way it was coming—a flood of sap!

Maybe Willy could go for help. But no—that

dog'd gotten himself all tangled up in the reins. What was I to do? Both my hands were more than full, pushing first one and then another wooden bucket under the spout, setting the full buckets on the sledge and then getting two more. Thinking fast, I leaned over and used my teeth to yank Willy free, all the while swinging buckets back and forth.

Spitting out the reins, I yelled, "Go home, Willy! Home. Get help!" And off he scooted, bounding up and down in the deep snow for all the world like one of those snowshoe rabbits. "Good old Willy. Will he do it?" I wondered. "Will he get help in time?"

By that time, I was plain tuckered out; my poor arms were so sore I could hardly move them. In fact, I discovered the next day that with all that lifting and lugging, both arms had stretched three inches. My left arm turned out to be half an inch longer than my right! Lulie had to sew strips of blanket material onto the sleeves of my jacket so that my wrists wouldn't freeze.

Now to this day, I don't know how Willy did it, but pretty soon I heard shouts, and there was Lulie followed by all you younguns to help out. Was I glad to see you! Pretty quick, everybody lined up, tallest to tiniest, and handed those heavy buckets off. Martha to April to William...one right after the other—a sap brigade.

Then a funny thing happened. The minute our very last bucket was filled, that big old maple gave a sort of hiccough—*errupp*—showering all of us with about nine bucketfulls of its watery sap, and quit. Yep, that stupendous stream of maple sap had run out! Not another drop.

Standing there, drenched and dripping with sap, I didn't rightly know whether to laugh or holler— laugh because I didn't have to lift one more heavy bucket or holler because the prodigious flow of sap had ceased.

Anyway, the sledge was so heavy with buckets of sap that poor old Macduff couldn't begin to budge it in the deep snow. Remember how all of us shoved and yanked and pushed and pulled and finally the sledge began to move? But it'd turned dark long before we got to the sugar shed.

Everybody pitched in and began dumping bucket after bucket of sap into our enormous kettle. Now I declare that kettle is big enough to hold Alston Crutchfield's oxen and three barn cats besides. Just the same, the kettle was overflowing before we'd emptied even the first row of buckets. Then we started in a-boiling and a-boiling the sap. Four days later, we were still at it, boiling down the sap from that mammoth maple to make syrup, boiling it some more to make maple sugar.

Now I never did go back and look for any more maple trees to tap that spring. Didn't need to. We had more sap—and syrup—than we knew what to do with! We had maple syrup on griddle cakes, on muffins, on cornmeal mush for breakfast; maple syrup on fried eggs, fritters, and pudding for lunch. And for dinner we had maple-baked ham and maple-stewed sweet potatoes with maple walnut pie for dessert. It got so that any time someone said "maple syrup" I got a sticky feeling in my throat and a sicky feeling in my stomach. You can see why I don't really like maple syrup anymore. Not even on snow!

P apa Alonzo appeared from the barn in time to hear the last of his story. "Maple syrup — bah!" he complained. "Right now, I have syrup stuck to my fingernails, gluing my eyelashes together, and…."

"But Papa…." Martha interrupted. Talking, not looking, she poured syrup until it drowned her pan-cakes and dripped onto the floor. Fast as melted butter, Willy scooted under the table and licked it up.

"But Papa Alonzo," Martha said, "Didn't you ever tap that big maple again?"

Papa Alonzo didn't reply until he'd washed his face and hands under the kitchen pump. Then he said, "Well, Martha, come May with all the snow melted, I took a walk in the woods. Wanted to see what that stupendous maple looked like all leafed out.

"At first, I couldn't find the tree. I searched and searched, but nowhere did I see any even half as large as the maple I'd tapped. And then I stumbled right over the place where the maple had stood. Yep, I found it. Actually, what I found wasn't the tree but a small heap of what looked like sawdust. When I picked up a pinch of it, however, I discovered it wasn't sawdust at all, but sugar, sweet maple sugar.

"That big old tree had pushed so hard and used up so much energy to give its last drop of sap that it simply self-destructed. Yep, it had boiled itself right down into a little mound of maple sugar."

Martha frowned. "Why didn't you bring the sugar home?"

Papa Alonzo shook his head. "You know, I was so tired of wrestling with those endless buckets and so tired of the smell of boiling sap that I didn't even bother to scoop it up. Probably, it's still there."

Martha giggled. "Unless the snowshoe rabbits ate it," she said. Even with Papa around, she always had the last word.

III.

The Gravel-Voiced Bear

When Papa Alonzo and Lulie started a family, Papa decided each baby girl's name should be akin to the month in which she was born. As he figured it, "Months are female—each one a beauty but a mite flighty and unpredictable." Lulie sniffed at that remark but went along with Papa's plan, except when the twins arrived.

Even Lulie had to admit the second Leatherby's name was most appropriate! As showery as the month in which she was born, April cried at everything. She cried when given the last ginger cooky, because they were all gone. She cried when Lulie gave her the first one; there might not be seconds. When happy, she cried tears of joy, and she wailed loudly when she was sad. What a stormsnickety child!

One spring day, April cried more than usual. She'd been in bed all week with tonsillitis and laryngitis, with beditis and boreditis—and a bad headache besides. Even Lulie's hot chicken broth didn't much help.

However, when Lulie handed her the soup, April

managed to croak "Thank you, Mama," her voice a
gravelly whisper.

Lulie smiled. "Nicely said. Being so polite, April,
you remind me of Papa Alonzo's sore throat and…."

"Have Papa come tell me the story," April begged
hoarsely, snuffling.

But Papa Alonzo couldn't oblige. That very morning he'd gone over the mountain to see what he could
see—besides the other side of the mountain!

"Never mind," Lulie said. "That story is one I
canned from the big snow. I'll go fetch it." April
stopped crying for one whole afternoon while she listened for the umpteenth time to the story of the
gravel-voiced bear.

Well, now, as I recollect…when Lulie and I
were first married, bears used to be thicker'n
bumblebees' fleas around here. They'd come right into
the fields and eat up the berries and beans without a
"please and thank you!" No manners at all! Leastwise
none to compare with Silas Grant, a paragon of polite-
ness. Silas called himself an "Equine Breeder"—his
fancied-up name for a horse trader.

Fiddleferns, but that man was a sight to ponder.
Skinny, turtle-mouthed, he dressed up in Sunday-go-
to-service fashion every day of the week, one of
Carroll County's leading citizens—self-appointed. A
most proper and polite gentleman, least-ways that's
how *he* put himself forth. Silas traveled to Boston once,

and ever after considered himself the County's champion expert on manners. He'd always "please, if you'll be so good as to" this and "thank you for your kind assistance" that. Humph! Silas was a persnickler and a bit of a phony, if you ask me, with his turned-out clothes and tucked-up airs. And he wasn't much as a judge of horses, either. But that was before....

Well, let's see. It must have been early April, a chilly, gray day that smelled like a late spring snow. I had a sore throat, felt like it was stuffed with red-hot popcorn. Lulie tried to convince me to stay home, but cousin Ezekiel Bean over to Conway told me Silas Grant had been talking up a horse he wanted to sell. I wanted a look at it, felt we needed another horse besides Macduff. I managed to hitch a ride with the post wagon heading that way.

But in spite of Silas Grant's fine talking, his horse turned out to be a dud, bedraggled and buckle-kneed. And swaybacked! When it trotted across the field, the grass tickled its belly and it set to hee-heeing hysterically. Silas had to dump a bucket of water over that nag's head to calm it down. Hardly good manners, I'd say! Of course, I was counting on riding home; but since I didn't buy the poor pitiful beast, I had to walk ten miles back through the forest.

Wouldn't you know it, about half-way home it began to rain, a nasty bone-chilling rain. Not a flowery April shower, no ma'am marigolds! Now I do a lot of tramping in the woods on my way from here to there, what with looking for firewood and trees for lumber, and I never know when I'm going to get caught out in a storm. So I've searched out some good shelters—caves, rock overhangs, and the like. Why, I even keep emergency food in them.

That wet April day, I hurried to my nearest shelter a step off the main path, stopping just long enough to fill my canteen from the spring. The shelter was a huge old hollow tree, almost big enough to hold the Saturday night square dance inside. I ducked in, shivering all over. Dad-rabbit, what I needed was something hot to drink! Reached up on the shelf I'd nailed there and pulled down my cache—a teapot and little tin of tea, some hard biscuits, and a pot of honey for sweetening.

Well, it took me a few false starts to get a small fire going on the dirt floor with the wood so damp and all, but finally the water I'd dipped out of the spring was a-boil. I threw in some tea, laid out some biscuits, and was just opening the pot of honey when I heard a noise.

Sort of a sniffly-snuffly noise, then a thump and a whump, and I looked nose to nose with the biggest black bear I'd ever encountered. Whooee, he was so close, I could feel his warm, smelly breath on my cheeks. Must've been about ten feet tall as he was rearing up at me.

I gave a little yelp and scrambled up inside the tree as fast as I could. That huge old tree was hollow way up into the top of it, thank the flies' eyes, and I shinnied up, double quick. Almost not quick enough

—the bear swiped at me with his foot-long claws. He missed me but got my britches. You can see where they're striped to this day. Corduroyed. I did manage to scoot up just beyond the reach of the bear. Well, I found a pretty solid place to cling to and sort of wedged myself in. I stared down and do you know what that bear was doing? He ignored me and without a "by your leave," hunkered himself right down beside my fire. First he nosed my mug of hot tea, tasted a biscuit, and then started in on the honey.

Now I was hopping mad and I shouted down in my crackledy voice, sort of sarcastic-like, "Hey, you there! Just invited yourself for tea, did you? Going to eat up my honey and biscuits without saying 'if you please'! Where are your manners, you impolite beast? You're—you're uncouth!"

And as I finished my yelling, I heard a sort of strangled yowl. I quick found a little knothole in the tree trunk and peeked outside. You won't believe what I saw—and heard!

There was Silas Grant, sitting astride that swaybacked nag, his face looking like wilted dandelions. He was opening and closing his mouth like a trout out of water, after which his teeth started clacking worse'n the rattlesnakes on Moat Mountain. I could hear him way up to where I was perched. Then Silas gave a little gasp.

"Please excuse me, Mr. Bear," he squawked. "I do not wish to offend you. Be so kind as to accept my apologies for interrupting your tea." Silas ducked his

head in a little jerking bow. By then the horse had con-
fronted the bear, too, and backed away. That nag got
its leg muscles a-moving, turned around, and started
running through the underbrush. Fast! Faster than I
thought such a sorry beast could move. Maybe I
should've bought the nag after all!

That big black bear got up, and I thought he was
going after Silas, maybe to shake hands, but no. Silas
Grant astride his buckle-kneed horse, along with his
uppity manners, evidently surprised the bear—or sat-
isfied any curiosity about tea parties, more likely.
Anyway, the bear shook his head back and forth, puz-
zled-like, and lumbered off in the opposite direction
from Silas Grant's undignified retreat.

Of course, I never did get my tea and honey that
day. I came home soaked to the skin and with a most
powerful cold. Lulie doctored me with a mustard plas-
ter and chicken soup. Just the same, I got laryngitis so
bad that for over a week I couldn't speak above a
whisper, and even whispering hurt. I couldn't tell
Lulie or anybody about Silas and the bear, and not
telling hurt worse'n my throat!

W ith the last words of the story, Papa Alonzo
appeared at the door.

"Papa Alonzo, whatever happened to that silly
man, Silas Grant?" April whispered.

Papa Alonzo pulled at his beard. "Well, I did hear
tell of him the next time I was over in Conway. As

people there piece it out, he came limping into the general store—must've been right after his tête á tête at my hollow tree. Silas' fine clothes were pulled every which way, a bit shredded-looking at the edges. And he began babbling away about a gravel-voiced bear who yelled at him for not having proper manners, a tea-drinking bear that catapulted his horse into conniptions.

"Of course, everybody in the general store started laughing and nudging each other. A gravel-voiced bear, indeed! And one with a taste for tea and good manners. Unbelievable! Besides, how could anyone, much less a bear, think Silas Grant was impolite? People in Conway all made so much fun of Silas that within the month he up and left town."

April croaked out, "Where'd he go?"

Papa Alonzo shrugged. "Some folks say he lit out for Ohio, some say Maine. But *I* heard he moved to Boston where probably even bears have good manners—if there are bears in Boston. Anyway, April, I haven't seen hat nor handkerchief of Silas since, much less his horse. Nor that bear, either."

IV.

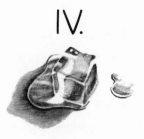

Willy's Ravenous Raccoons

T he third Leatherby, William, was a worry-wart, any angle you viewed him. He did more winkling and wankling every day than most ten-year-olds do in nine months of mosquitoes! When the sun was out strong, William worried that Polliwog Pond would dry up. When it rained, he was sure the Pond would flood.

Mealtimes, William worried that he wouldn't get as much corn chowder as his brother, Fletcher. Or else he was sure he couldn't eat all Lulie dished up.

One day, William was watching Willy, Papa Alonzo's old dog, sleep. His feet jerked back and forth, for all the world as though running up Blacktop Mountain.

"Mama, what's the matter with Willy?" William asked, biting his lip. "He's twitching all over."

"Just dreaming, William," Lulie replied. "Maybe wanting to go with Papa Alonzo."

"Where's Papa?" William asked.

"In the south field, dusting the corn shucks with

sugar so's the ears'll grow extra sweet this year."

"But bees love sugar. Papa'll get stung!"

Lulie sighed. "Stop fussling, youngun! Go to the pantry and find the jar labeled WILLY. It'll give you something to do besides niggling me."

When William returned with the large jar, Lulie undid the lid and the first sentences slipped out.

W ell, now, as I recollect…Willy, here, when he was young, could chase the brass buttons off the jacket of Mrs. Whitmore's boy, Warty, and outrace a rattlesnake up Moat Mountain. Just look at him now—an old hound, lazy and slow and broader than a peck basket. Yet that dog wasn't any bigger'n a turnip when I found him.

I'd been over to Miz Cotton's place that spring, helping raise a new barn. Coming home, slipping through the woods as quiet as a luna moth, I heard a little whimpering sound. Peeked over a fallen oak tree and could hardly believe my eyes. There was a little black pup snuggling up to a fat raccoon and her mothering it. A puppy! And me needing a new dog after Shep disappeared.

Now that Shep was a good dog—too good! Best sheepdog in Carroll County. I'd yell "Fetch!" and he'd round up a whole flock of fifty sheep, march them to pasture single file with the shortest lamb in front and the tallest ram bringing up the rear.

And cows! I'd say "Fetch" and Shep'd get them

from the upland pasture and into their stalls before I had time to grab a milkpail and plomp down on my three-legged stool.

Well, one day when Shep'd been working extra hard, I thought that dog should play a pidgewidget. So I tossed him a big stick and yelled "Catch!" But Shep must've thought I said "Fetch"—he took off into the woods like a double-jointed jackrabbit. Before I could whistle Dixie, he was back with another stick, bigger'n the first one, laid it at my feet, and dashed off again. And came back with another, and another and another, each stick bigger'n the last. Finally, after lugging back a log so large he could barely get his teeth around it, Shep disappeared. Never did return—that dog must have thought he should fetch home the whole forest and was too embarrassed to face me when he found he couldn't do it.

Willy, here, is a different wag of the tail. He's smart, all right, and good-hearted; but even when he was young and spry, Willy couldn't fetch feathers from a wet hen.

Anyway, on the day I found the big mother raccoon taking care of him, I picked up that black pup and brought him right home for Lulie to mother. We'd have a dog again! Never *did* find the puppy's mother—probably cornered by a bear.

What with all the chores that spring and caring for all you younguns, we didn't have time to name the pup. Just called him "dog." But "dog" doesn't fit very well in the mouth whenever anyone wants to yell,

"Hey, dog, here, dog!" Besides which, every time we yelled, "Come, dog," our old sow, Winnie, must of thought we said, "Come, hog!" She and her litter of piglets would tramp over the pigsty fence and appear at the kitchen door, oinking for food. Pretty quick, we knew we needed to go whole-hog and find a proper canine name for our dog. But what name?

Now every time Lulie set the food in front of you children, she poured some into a big bowl for the puppy and put it out on the back stoop. And when she went to get the bowl, it was always licked cleaner than a clamshell, with the black pup whimpering for more. Lulie'd sigh and say, "Will he ever get filled up?" and later, "Will he ever stop eating?" It was hard enough to keep you younguns fed, but me-oh-magpie, to have a bottomless-belly of a pup!

The weeks flapped by, and Lulie would look at that skinny little pup, shake her head, and say "Will he ever grow?" And after each feeding, she'd bring in the empty bowl from the back stoop and mutter, "Will he ever get enough to eat? Will he?"

Then one evening in early June, Lulie went out back and plunked down the bowl as usual. She was tick-tuckered out that day and when she noticed an extravagant sunset just catching fire in the west, she stayed at the door, all peaceful-like, to watch. Imagine her amazement when she heard the puppy give a little yippety-yap and around the corner came a fat raccoon with nine babies trailing after her! Those critters went right over to the bowl and lapped it slick-slack clean while that dog danced around the raccoons, as much as to say "Be my guests!"

Of course, the nine baby raccoons were cunning, with their little black-masked faces and their little paws holding on to the edge of the bowl to keep from sliding in. But raccoons, grown up, would strip the corn from the stalks and steal apples from our orchard. Corn and apples we needed to feed *you* nine little ones. In fact, one of the reasons we had a dog was to chase raccoons from the garden!

Lulie called softly for the rest of us to come look, and we got to the door just in time to see ten raccoons turn striped-tail and march off into the woods. Lulie laughed a little, patted the puppy and said, "Will he ever be any use around here? Will he?"

You younguns laughed, too, and began to chorus, "Will he? Will he? Will he?" And that little black dog began to jump and yip and chase his tail, as if to say "That's my name!" And from that day to this, our dog has answered to "Willy."

W illy jumped up with a loud "Rauw woof!" just as Papa Alonzo walked in the door.

"Papa Alonzo," William said, looking worried. "Was *I* named after Willy?"

"Nope—after your great-grandaddy, William Leatherby, who could cut up a log quicker than a pair of beavers. Always used a two-man saw—all by himself!"

"Did Willy's raccoons eat up all the sweet corn so we won't have any?"

"What a worry-woggle you are, William! Well, come early last August I was out in the corn patch, feeling the ears, trying to find some big enough to pick. All of us hankered for sweet corn. Willy came snuffling along and then stopped, rigid as a bean pole. I looked up to see a passel of raccoons—nine half-grown ones and their mother—standing alongside the corn stalks looking hungry. Hankering for sweet corn, too! Whoops, I thought. Now what will that dog do? Will he chase them away?"

"Did he?" William asked, scratching behind Willy's ears.

"Nope, Willy sat whap-dab down in front of those animals. Still as a wood tick, he stared into each black-masked face, one after the other, and the ten raccoons stared back at Willy. Then he must of made up his mind...gave a couple of wags and woofs and one long howl. Believe it or not, those raccoons turned around and disappeared into the woods. What'd Willy tell them? Who knows! But to this very day, we've never lost a single ear of corn nor one apple. Not yet."

"But Mama says the food in Willy's bowl on the back stoop still vanishes," William said, "in what she calls a most astonishing way!"

V.

Summer Soup

"**A** flibbertijibbet!" That's what Lulie called Fletcher, the fourth Leatherby. "A perpetual motion machine." If Fletcher wasn't climbing up a tree, he was running down a hill. If he wasn't hopping circles around the kitchen table, he was climbing the ladder to the hayloft.

The only time Fletcher stood still was when he shot arrows from an old bow that once belonged to Papa's Great-uncle Quimby. Fletcher shot arrows at everything—dahlias and dragonflies, frogs and fiddle-head ferns. Even Winnie's piglets. Fortunately, Fletcher's flying missiles always missed.

But one hot summer day, even nine-year-old Fletcher sat very still. "Whip-de-doo, it's too hot to spit!" he complained. "And too hot to move a muscle."

All the Leatherby younguns, stretched out every which way on the grass, stared into the maple tree overhead. Not one wisp of wind twiggled the leaves.

Suddenly, Fletcher leaped to his feet. "Hey—the

ice house!" he yelled. "I bet the ice blocks Papa
Alonzo cut and stored last winter haven't all melted.
Ice would cool us off!"

Eight voices called out, "Go look, Fletcher."

Lulie, sitting on the doorstep shelling peas,
echoed, "Go look, Fletcher."

Fletcher ran down the path to the ice house. In a
few seconds he was back, holding a smallish lump of
knobbly ice, dripping, in his hot hands. As the ice
thawed and evaporated, to everyone's amazement,
words began to drift in the hazy air and settle into sentences. Another of Papa Alonzo's frozen stories! All
about how hot it was when Papa was a boy.

N owadays, the whole world seems to be cool-
ing off—winters getting colder and summers
nowhere near as hot as when I was a youngun. No,
sirree. Well, now, as I recollect...the summer I turned
seven and stood about as tall as a bear's belly button
was a real dingdonger! Still, that summer had started
out just like always, with June flowers and showers,
rows of asparagus, wild strawberries tucked among
the field grasses.

My Daddy planted his cornfields right on sched-
ule and by July the stalks were higher than a cow's
horn. In the vegetable garden, peas, beans, tomatoes
all stretched right up toward the sun. But then, mid-
July or so, things began to go green-gopher wrong.

One morning the sun rose as usual, round and red, arching up until it was hanging right overhead — a hot, sticky, July noon.

Yep, but that day the sun must have melted onto the roof of the sky, or something. It got stuck! Two o'clock, three o'clock came and we didn't much notice. But long about five-thirty, when the sun should have been tipping over the western hills, we knew something was wrong. Instead of setting, bringing a cool evening breeze, the sun just beat down hotter and hotter.

Why, it was so hot that when my Mama sent me out to pick raspberries for supper, I discovered they'd cooked down into raspberry jam. And the apples in the orchard had stewed themselves into apple sauce — would you believe it?

But that wasn't all, not by a berry basket! The sun never did set — just glared down all night long, making it mighty hard to sleep. Then along about midnight a loud bang-bang, rat-a-tat-tat knocked us spang out of bed. Fireworks? But the Fourth of July was last week, and hunting season wouldn't begin for months. We ran to the windows. There in the west field, the corn Daddy planted was popping — exploding right off the stalks!

We ate and ate until we felt *we'd* pop, but the corn still was piled head high. Daddy had to do something. He hitched up our old mule, Maggoty, to the plow, trying to clear that field. But no use — those white kernels just bounced up and popped right back down on the field. Daddy had to give up. Of course, those huge popcorn drifts didn't melt, so we had a long white winter—from July on! It wasn't until February, right after Valentine's Day, in fact, that winter winds blew away the last kernels.

But back in July, day after day was just the same—hours of sun stuck overhead. The hens lay in the shade instead of laying eggs and I had to search hard to find any. Mama meant to scramble eggs for breakfast, but when she cracked them, every single egg was hard-boiled. So we ate egg salad.

The whole garden stewed under that blazing sun. Why for lunch we ate hot tomato soup, squeezed into our bowls right from the vine, along with new potatoes roasted in the ground and peas boiled in their pods. And Mama didn't have to fire up the stove to bake a pie. She just rolled out a pie crust, stood under the peach tree, and shook the branches a little. Peaches plopped down, soft and hot, and her pie was ready for dessert!

When I went fishing down by the brook, I didn't need to bait my fishhook. Nope, all I had to do was to hold out a fry pan. The brook must have been too hot to swim in, because trout just leaped into my pan, fried crisp and brown and ready to eat.

Of course, it was mighty hard to figure out night from day, and we all hankered for a good night's sleep. The birds never quit singing, for one thing, and after a few days they sounded plumb worn out. Ever heard a tired robin? Instead of chirping "Cheery-up," they squawked "Go-to-bed."

Then, too, none of the night owls ever gave a hoot, just slept. Mice multiplied so fast that our seven cats ran ragged keeping the furry little critters from holing up in the cheese or burrowing into Mama's bread.

Anyway, every day we felt hotter and tireder and crosser, just aching for dark and a cool breeze. But no, that big red balloon of a sun stayed stuck smick-smack overhead. We began to lose track of what hour or day it was. Everyone grumbled, "We have to do something about that sun!" But what?

Then one day, stretched out under the big maple tree trying to catch a little shade and a snooze, I had an idea. Running into the storage shed, I rummaged through "keep it, we might need it" piles of junk until I found Great-uncle Quimby's old bow and arrow — the one he'd used to stop the meanest black bear in Carroll County when it was fixing to gobble up his brother, Isaac. I tied a long string to the arrow, figured I'd try aiming for the sun. Maybe I could get a nick, grab the string, and tug that hot ball toward the west.

Fitting the arrow into the huge bow, I pulled back on the bowstring, back, back until my arm quivered like fish eggs in the pond. Whingo! That arrow rose up through the air faster'n a frog snaps up a fly. Praying I wouldn't get sizzled so close to the sun, I grabbed onto the string and rode it to high heaven. But I'd failed! We didn't hit the sun. Instead, that arrow arched way over the horizon and just kept going — with me in tow.

After a few seconds — *whomp*! It hit smack into

Venus. But Great-uncle Quimby's arrow didn't stop
there. It pierced through one after another of the planets—Mars, Jupiter, Pluto—skewering the whole
bunch together. Then, with a sort of whoo-ooshy
sound, it hit the full moon sailing up from the east.
Imagine—that arrow had punctured the whole solar
system! All this time, I'm hanging on for dear dia-
monds at the tag-end, feeling moonstruck!

And then the moon itself struck. Trailing the long
stringtail of celestial bodies—and me—the moon
bumped blang into that big old sun, gave it a shove
and...suffering Saturn! The sun began to move. At
last. It slid farther and farther toward the west and
finally set in a blast of pinkish-purplish orange. I guess
the whole solar system was mighty bored with being
stuck in orbit...or maybe miffed at the sun's laziness.

What about me? Well, that string broke just as we
sailed over Laurel Lake. I fell a long fall, but, thank my
lucky stars, water made for soft landing. Cooled me off
considerably besides. All the planets rolled away, too,
like a broken string of pearls, and settled back into
their own orbits.

Glad to be back home, I breathed a sigh of relief
and headed for bed. The whole world needed a good
night's sleep for a change. Around midnight I was
awakened by a whippoorwill's call. I looked out my
window and there was the moon, round and proud, as
if to say, "Look at me—I did it! With a little help from
you." Of course I never did find out what happened to
that arrow. If anyone ever flies as far as the moon,

maybe they'll find it there—Great-uncle Quimby's
arrow.

J ust before the tale ended, Papa Alonzo
appeared from the garden where he'd been
trampling tomato worms and squishing squash bee-
tles. Mopping his face with his bandana, he
complained, "It's hotter than a horned toad's hang-
nail!"

"The sun must be stuck again," Fletcher said.

Papa Alonzo chuckled. "I wonder. Of course, up
'til now, from that day to this, the sun has followed its
usual routine—always nudged by the moon. Stuck
again? Doesn't seem likely.

"You know, younguns, sometimes I like to think
back on that summer. Mighty hot and uncomfortable,
true, but every now and then I get a hankering for
sun-fried trout, tomato soup and boiled peas from the
garden. And for dessert—hot peach pie, fresh off the
tree."

He looked around. "Now where in the zing-zodiac
did Fletcher go?"

The twins pointed. "Over there," they chorused.

Silhouetted against the late afternoon glow,
Fletcher was shooting arrow after arrow toward the
sun. With a long string tied to each one.

VI.

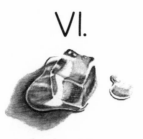

The Day the Goat
Turned Blue

T he Leatherby twins, Jemma and Jethro, were double trouble from the day they were born. They fought twice as much and yelled twice as loud as most younguns. When Jemma yelled at Jethro, her voice could start an avalanche on Ragged Mountain. When Jethro yelled back, all the crows in the cornfield headed for Delaware.

Besides, each twin ate twice as much as any other seven-year-old in Carroll County. When Lulie baked bread, Jemma and Jethro ate a loaf apiece. When she baked a bushel of beans on Saturday night, the twins ate up the leftovers intended for Sunday lunch, then yelled for more.

Early one September Saturday, Lulie was near-frantic getting all the Leatherbys ready to leave for the Sanborn Fair. Seven of 'em were lined up, hair slicked, shoes shiny with spit and polish. But Jemma and Jethro were still fighting and yelling. And eating muffin after muffin.

"I swear," Lulie said, "You two are worse then our

goat, Sundew, and he ate everything he could fit in his mouth."

"We want to hear Papa Alonzo's story!" shouted Jethro.

"About Sundew turning blue!" Jemma shrieked.

But Papa Alonzo was outside polishing up the pumpkins and fluffing the ducklings to show at the Sanborn Fair, hoping to win a blue ribbon or two for the Leatherby farm.

Lulie went to the pantry and brought back a jar. "Here's Papa's tale about Sundew. Sure hope it'll keep you quiet while you finishing eating." She unscrewed the lid and the tale began.

B lueberry pie? My favorite dessert! Eating a wedge dripping with blueberry juice always reminds me of the day one of our goats turned blue. Yep, blue as pie! Well, now, as I recollect...it was Sundew. You kiddies remember Sundew—our white goat named for the fuzzy little plant growing all over the old meadow where it's too wet to mow.

The sundew is an odd plant—it eats bugs, traps them on its sticky leaves. And our white goat ate everything and anything, just as if things stuck to his tongue. Why, set down a milk pail for one second to scratch a mosquito bite and Sundew would gulp it down—drain that pail to the last drop, then begin to chomp on the pail itself.

Drop a mitten and before you could lean over to

pick it up, Sundew would chew it to shreds. He gobbled everything in sight. We tried tying him, but he ate
the rope. We tried putting him in a pen, but he chewed
through the wooden slats before we got the last board
nailed on. Anything small enough to fit into his mouth,
Sundew ate it. Until one September....

September first and fair time, it was—the Sanborn
Fair. As folks around here would have it, the biggest
one-day fair in New England. People drove in from
miles around, their carts and buggies piled to the
clouds with kiddies and wives and things to show off.
Maybe win a prize. They brought potatoes as big as
barrels, pumpkins Cinderella could ride in without a
fairy godmother's wand, string beans so long and
strong they could've been used to tame a mountain
lion.

And the womenfolk bringing quilts and aprons
and knitted whatevers, proving how busy they'd been
last winter, all looking for first prize ribbons. Blue ribbons. Yep, that's what all of us wanted to win—for
Best Chocolate Cake, Best Canned Beets, Most
Beautiful Quilt, for Strongest Team of Oxen, Biggest
Hubbard Squash, Best Breeding Sow.

Well, now, the Sanborn Fair was an exciting time,
believe you me! Lulie and I were just like every other
farm family. Long about the middle of August every
year, we'd try to decide what we'd grown that might
bring *us* a blue ribbon. A ten-dollar bill went along

with that strip of blue silk, a prize not to be sneezed at,
I'll tell the whole county!

So anyway, I said to Lulie, "How about it? What
are we going to enter in the Sanborn Fair this year?"

She sort of waggled her head and wiggled her
nose and allowed as how she'd have to think on it.
Last January, Lulie'd half-finished piecing together a
Snow on the Mountain quilt. But one of you little ones
neglected to latch the front door heading off to school
one day. Sundew nosed it open and finished the quilt
for Lulie. Finished it off, I should say.

In our garden, cabbages grew as big as water-
melon, but worms had nibbled tunnels into the best
ones. Cucumbers were lumpy, the squash lop-sided.
As for our sow, Winnie, and her last litter—have you
ever seen pigeon-toed piglets? Right off hand, we
couldn't think of anything good enough to enter for a
prize that year.

So what were we going to do? Lulie looked as
glum as a gopher with gout. Not entering something
at the Fair was like discovering our offspring—all
nine of 'em—turned out to be horse thieves. Besides,
as I reminded Lulie, "We've won at least one blue ribbon every single year since we got hitched and started
farming the place. Oh, except for that one year you
had the twins and I sprained my ankle chasing
Sundew out of the blueberry bushes. That goat always
craves blueberries."

Hey—blueberry bushes. That was it! Plump and
juicy, silvery-blue, our berries were bigger this year

than we'd ever seen them. Larger than Mrs. Wittemore's down the road a piece and a lot larger than the ones in Jasper Jenkins' patch up on Varnum Notch. I'd checked. Sneaked in when Jasper was over in Center Rockton for a wedding.

Just before the fair, Lulie and I cleaned up our best-looking baskets and went out to pick blueberries. But that ding-dratted goat! Sundew had eeled his way out of the barn where I'd taken to shutting him up. When we got to the patch, he was chomping on the fattest, most perfect berries. Would you believe it! And nibbling on the blue chicory flowers growing near the bushes—for salad, I guess. But he'd eaten a good half of the berries—gallons of them. Lulie declared, "I swear, Sundew, you're going to turn blue!" But he didn't. Not then.

I shut Sundew in the barn again and Lulie and I set to work stripping off those big round berries and plopping them into our baskets. And every now and then picking a smaller one for our mouths. Soon our baskets were heaping. They sure looked good enough to win a prize. And maybe Lulie'd enter some of her canned fruit or pickles.

Early the morning of the fair, we hitched up Macduff to the wagon and counted off you Leatherbys—yep, nine of you—to make sure we hadn't forgotten anyone. We also made sure the twins weren't within arm's reach of the food! Then we set out for Sanborn with four baskets of blueberries, three shiny jars of peaches, two less-than-perfect bushels of potatoes, and—oh, yes—Sundew.

Sundew? Now we hated to admit it, but when Lulie and I took a second look at our livestock, we agreed that he was the best-looking animal on the place. Plump, of course, bright-eyed, narrow-hoofed. We scrubbed him and brushed his white coat until it gleamed, although it took all of us—me, Lulie, and all nine of you—to do the job. We even brushed his teeth to erase the blueberry stains. And Sundew did look elegant with his hoofs trimmed, his horns polished and tied with blue yarn. Blue? A pinch of wishful thinking that the goat'd win us a blue ribbon.

We tied Sundew to the back of the wagon and set off. And to make a long story short, or at any rate, shorter, I should say, we had a good day. Of course, Sundew chewed himself loose and managed to swallow down most of the plums Ezekiel Bean had exhibited in the food display, then overturned a table loaded with glasses of jam.

And during the kids' Blueberry Pie Eating Contest, Sundew butted in and ate up a pie so fast he almost won. He came in second to "Barrels" Boyd who can swallow a six-inch pie in six seconds. Jemma and Jethro weren't speedy enough to win, but they ate four apiece, which Judge Carter called some kind of record.

Now Sundew didn't win a blue ribbon. I suspect the head judge didn't take kindly to the fact that our goat bit a chunk out of his hat when he leaned over to inspect Sundew's hoofs. But in the end, we did take away two blue ribbons and two ten-dollar bills — Hooray! One for our blueberries and one for Lulie's peaches.

Proud as parsnips, we tacked our two blue ribbons to the front of the wagon and started for home, already spending the prize money about a dozen different ways.

Ah, yes, I know. I still haven't told about when the goat turned blue. Nope, it wasn't Molly Dodge's blueberry jam Sundew ate, glass jars and all, nor was it Miz Mowatt's blueberry pie he'd swallowed whole before the judges could taste it. And it wasn't our own prize blueberries which he gobbled up when our backs were turned that did the trick. Nope, Sundew was still a mostly white goat when we arrived home that evening, a bit blue-stained around the edges, of course, and with his stomach considerably fatter than when we'd started off that morning.

I was just lifting down baby Moses who'd long since fallen asleep when I heard Lulie yell, "Oh, no! Sundew, stop it, you old goat. You are going to turn blue!"

Believe it or not, that goat had gnawed through his rope again and was at the front of the wagon with you twins. I turned around just in time to see you each grab the end of a blue ribbon in a tug-of-war with Sundew. The goat was winning.

And Lulie was right. As the last fragments of our

first-prize ribbons disappeared between his teeth,
Sundew *was* turning blue. First, his head and shoulders, then his front legs. As I watched, the color
inched toward his middle and kept moving back until
even his tail was blue! I guess you'd have to say that
Sundew turned out to be a blue ribbon goat, after all.
Well, anyway, a blue goat. And that's the truth of the
matter.

J ust as the tale ended, Papa Alonzo and Lulie
returned from loading the wagon for the fair.
Jemma and Jethro yanked each others' hair, then
smiled, the picture of innocence. But the story of
Sundew had quieted them. In a soft voice, Jemma
begged, "Papa, before we leave, tell what made
Sundew white again!"

"You, two!" Papa Alonzo sighed. "Well, Sundew
didn't turn white when Jemma lathered his hair with
laundry soap and Jethro dragged him into the brook.
And the goat stayed blue when you two dusted him
with flour. Of course, the stuff dried like cement and
we had to chisel it off so's he could move.

"As I recollect, it was the day you hauled Sundew
into our bedroom and held him up to the dresser mir-
ror. That goat was so shocked, looking at his blueness,
that his hair turned white with fright.

"In fact, Sundew was so white that last winter
during the big snow we couldn't tell where his ears
began and where his tail stopped. Come spring, about

the time the snowshoe rabbits left for the woods, that pesky creature up and disappeared."

"Maybe he ran off to join the rabbits," Jemma said.

Jethro added, "Maybe he turned color like the rabbits do in the spring."

"Jethro and I did see a strange-looking brown deer last week," Jemma said.

Jethro shouted, "Chewing on that old tin wash-tub behind the barn!"

"Maybe it was Sundew!" they yelled.

VII.

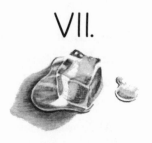

Put Her in a Pumpkin Shell

U nder a harvest moon, there was a snap to the air and the scurry of dead leaves unsettled by the wind. Winter was just around the corner. Papa Alonzo had labored all day, chinking up cracks and stuffing crevices with rags, making boots for the cows and earmuffs for the pigs. After supper, he leaned back in his big chair.

"I'm as tagragged as last summer's scarecrow!" he said, yawning. "We'll get a heavy frost tonight, or my name isn't Alonzo Leatherby."

Lulie knew that most of the crops were harvested and stored for the winter, but she was worried. She jabbed at the mitten she was knitting. "Will a frost harm that pile of pumpkins by the woodshed?" she asked.

"Oh, I covered them with Macduff's old horse blanket. Can't have you younguns howling your ears off because you don't have a jack-o-lantern." Papa Alonzo laughed.

At the word "jack-o-lantern," Octava's head popped up from the basket of popcorn ears she and

44

the twins were rubbing together, sliding off the kernels. The twins nudged Octava. With her sixth
birthday on Halloween, she was a born trick-or-
treater. And right now it was…trick time! She ducked
down and snuck out of the room. In three whisks of a
broom, Octava was back from the pantry with a jar.
She dumped its contents into the basket.

Papa Alonzo and Lulie both sat up stiff as wash-
boards, startled, when a deep voice boomed out of the
basket, rattling the popcorn ears. Nearly smothered
by children's giggles, the Halloween story began.
Papa Alonzo looked at Lulie, grinned, and settled
back to listen to himself tell the tale.

W ell, now, as I recollect…my little sister, your
Aunt Octavie, was only six at the time, but as
sharp as a two-tined fork. Born on Halloween,
Octavie was as full of spunk and spittle as a beaver
trying to dam up the Merrimack River at flood stage.
I was mostly grown, doing a man's work with my
daddy by then.

That year everything in our garden grew bigger
and better than ever before—or since. Why, we had
three-foot-long carrots and onions as big as cannon-
balls. And corn! Those ears were so heavy that the
stalks arched right over into the ground and rooted.
Corn bridges, you might say, so sturdy you could walk
right up and over them to the next row. Great on
muddy days.

In fact, those ears were so large that my Mama'd cook just two ears of corn for the whole family. One for her and Daddy and one for us kiddies to share. Mama'd slather on the butter and salt, then line us up—girls at one end and boys at the other. When Daddy said "Go!" everyone'd eat as fast as greased lightning. And we didn't stop until we met in the middle—boys against girls.

But the most amazing thing we grew that summer was a pumpkin. Now back in the spring, after the last frost, we dug up a small patch out near the woodshed and pushed in some pumpkin seeds. It wasn't but a few days until a vine was growing there as big around as my arm. And blossoms! They were so huge that every time it rained, I just moseyed over and picked a blossom to keep me dry while I slopped the pigs and lugged milk pails. Better than any umbrella.

We could hardly wait to see what kind of pumpkins we'd get during such a great growing year. And grow, those pumpkins did! I swear they looked larger every time I walked past the woodshed. A bumper crop.

Long about October, Daddy and I hitched up our mule, Maggoty, and we dragged all those huge pumpkins over to the root cellar. A mighty full root cellar, crowded with bushels of oversized carrots, squash, and potatoes. It was hard to close the door after we rolled in those pumpkins.

One pumpkin, though, was too big to bring in. It was so gigantic that Maggoty couldn't begin to haul it anywhere. Why, I don't think Wesley Cook's double team of oxen would have been able to budge that pumpkin. So there it sat, round and orange and enormous, nearly as large as the woodshed.

Well, one Saturday near the end of October, almost Halloween time, when the air and ground both crackled with frost, my sister, Octavie, looked out the window and said, "Let's make our jack-o-lantern today."

"Sure thing." "Why not!" "Can we?" Everyone yelled at once.

Pointing at that enormous pumpkin by the woodshed, Octavie added, "I want a jack-o-lantern made out of *that* pumpkin!"

And what a jack-o-lantern it would be! The trouble was, how could anyone cut the top off and carve out a face? We talked the problem up and down and all around Robinson's barn until finally I allowed as how I could get a ladder and the crosscut saw to cut off the top.

"But," I said, "Someone else'll have to carve the face. I can't take the time. What with all the harvesting chores before snowfall, Daddy needs my help."

Of course, it was Octavie who said, "I'm going to do the carving!"

Everyone agreed that such an extraordinary jack-o-lantern would make it the best Halloween ever!

Now back in those days, young folk did indeed play tricks on Halloween, sometimes even mean tricks—letting the bull out of the pasture, overturning outhouses, and the like. Treats were for the little ones.

Why, I recollect the time a gang of boys over Fahey Hollow way stole Abe Quimby's mail box and carted it six miles away where they stuck it right next to Mathilda Weed's. Now everyone in Carroll County knew Abe had been sneaking looks at Mathilda Weed for nigh onto ten years, but never had the jump-and-ginger to do more than look. Abe Quimby was so embarrassed he finally made a move—to Rhode Island, with Mathilda Weed as his wife.

Next Halloween those Fahey Hollow rowdies coaxed Gardner Elliott's Holstein cow into the White Church and pulled her right up the stairs to the steepletop. She grabbed the bell rope, and when it started bonging, the silly cow got so scared she wouldn't budge. Gardner had to rig up ropes and pulleys and enlist the whole township to help lower her. And from then on, that Holstein refused to give a drop of milk on Sundays once the church bell started to ring.

Anyway, the year of the great pumpkin, the Fahey Hollow gang was still around, causing a ruckus here and there, scaring the more timid of the populace. Octavie and my other little sisters and brothers worried a whole lot about what those rowdies might do to the huge pumpkin, but they wanted it made into a jack-o-lantern, just the same.

So on the Saturday before Halloween, I hauled out

the ladder, got the saw, and did the job. I'd just slid the cut-off top aside when Jeb Cooper came riding up, all of a-lather, and yelled that the Town Hall was afire and every able-bodied man needed to put it out. I climbed down from that pumpkin quick as a squirrel flicks its tail, hitched up Maggoty, and Daddy and I headed for town.

Octavie'd been watching me, of course. Always busy as a pan of corn popping, she could hardly wait to carve that broad pumpkin face. Well, she decided to climb up the ladder and look inside that pumpkin. Once she got to the top, somehow or other her foot skidded—you know how slippery pumpkin pulp is— and *whomp*! She fell right smack into the middle of that fat pumpkin. At the same time, the ladder slid off and fell to the ground. Thud!

Now Octavie wasn't hurt, only her dignity, but nobody was there to take notice except for the pumpkin seeds. So she sat a spell, thinking what to do. She tried to pull herself out, but her arms weren't long enough. She tried jumping and grabbing, but she was too short. She tried yelling, but with the top still mostly covering the opening, her voice sounded muffled and damped, even to her.

After awhile, Octavie got tired, so she cleaned off some pumpkin seeds and sat down, maybe dozed a little. Then she tried yelling again, but that was as useless as buying shoes for a centipede. What should she do? She knew that Mama would think she'd gone with Daddy and me—she often did—and it might be

a long time before anyone would begin looking for
her. Now Octavie wasn't the crying kind, but just the
same she reached in her pinafore pocket for a hanky,
in case. And what did she find but her sewing scissors
that she always carried! Hadn't given them a thought
before, but maybe, just maybe, she could cut a hole
big enough to yell through so someone in the house
would hear her.

She stuck the scissors in the thick flesh of the
pumpkin and pushed and pushed. Finally she cut a
circle, big and round, but when she knocked out the
piece of pumpkin, she saw she'd made a mistake. The
hole was on the side facing the barn, not where anybody'd be likely to hear her at that hour.

So she set out to carve a second circle. This time,
she managed to make an opening toward the house.
But yell and scream and shout as loud as she could, no
one answered her cries.

It was nearing sundown, and cold. Octavie was
getting just a little scared. What if she had to stay
there all night? But she set her lips together in a firm
line and said, "Well! I made one big round hole and
then another. Maybe I can find a way to cut myself out
of this pumpkin shell!"

Her legs were tired, so Octavie sat down. She
sawed and sawed with her sharp scissors. A big job,
but finally she managed to carve a hole wide enough
so that maybe, just maybe, she could crawl out.

About that time she heard a noise—a sneaky,
snickery noise—and a low chuckle and whisper. The

noise scared Octavie for a second. Then she decided it must be some of her brothers and sisters, doing the evening chores. Or maybe Daddy and I'd returned.

"Help! Help! Pull me out of this pumpkin!" Octavie yelled as loudly as she could—and Octavie never was known for having a quiet voice. She heard a gasp, and voices, excited like.

"What's that?"

"I'm getting out of here!"

"Jumping Juniper Berries!"

Then what sounded like running.

Right about that time, we drove Maggoty up to the barn, mighty startled, let me tell you, to see a small figure all covered with stringy orange come running toward us—and right after we'd passed the Fahey Hollow Bunch tearing down the road looking like they'd seen the ghost of Hanging Judge Calkins!

Well, when Daddy and I got done telling Octavie and she got done telling us and we got done telling the whole family what had happened, we laughed until we cried.

We all trouped out to that enormous pumpkin and started laughing all over again. Yep, those holes that Octavie had cut looked just like two round eyes and a wide slash of a mouth—a perfect jack-o-lantern!

O ctava jumped up and down. "My favorite story!" she said. "I like it 'cause Aunt Octavie's name is almost the same as mine. And we

were both Halloween babies!" Then she looked
scared. "But Papa, maybe that gang will smash our
pumpkins this year."

"No way to Saint's Day!" Papa Alonzo said. "We
heard tell that the Fahey Hollow gang spread the
word, trying to scare folks about a haunted jack-o-
lantern. Of course Daddy and I made parsnip- certain
all of Carroll County heard the truth about that haunted pumpkin—how a little girl had scared the
suspenders off those big bullies. And you know, that
was the last time those rowdies went out tricking on
Halloween. Too embarrassed to face the populace, I'd
surmise."

Octava grinned, a wide pumpkin grin. "Well, I'm
ready to go carve a jack-o-lantern." She reached in her
apron pocket and pulled out her sewing scissors. "And
maybe haunt it!"

VIII.

Talking Turkey

T hanksgiving Day. The kitchen was bursting with the aroma of roasting meat and bubbling sauces. It was stuffed to overflowing with Lulie and nine hungry Leatherby younguns. In the back yard, Papa Alonzo was splitting wood. He sniffed the air and said, "Those delicious smells! I'm hungry enough to chew the nails out of a rail fence!"

In the kitchen fixing dinner, Lulie was as busy as an octopus with triplets. Shadowing her every move, the eighth Leatherby, Novia, tugged at Lulie's apron. "Where do pickles come from?" she asked. "Why are cranberries red? What makes vinegar sour? Are mushrooms fairy umbrellas? Who gets to pull the wishbone? When do we eat?" Novia was one big question mark!

Lulie sighed, hands on hips. "I'm fed up. Novia, no more questions! Quit poking the pudding and dibbling in the cranberry sauce. Go help your sisters and brothers." And she turned back to stirring the gravy.

A loud crash and a voice wailing, "I just wanted to

help," brought the whole family to the pantry door. Novia stood staring at the broken jar on the floor, crying as only a four-year-old can cry. Then her sobs stopped abruptly. From the jar's remnants arose Papa Alonzo's tale about Thanksgiving—and turkeys.

⬡⬡⬡

T urkeys are tough birds, all right, although carving one up to eat on Thanksgiving is popular with folks nowadays. Well, now, as I recollect ...back when you older kiddies weren't much higher than a milk pail, we *didn't* eat turkey, no-ma'am-mumpkin! Every Thanksgiving Lulie would go pick out our fattest hen to roast. But one year I decided to get us something special for that special day—a Thanksgiving turkey.

Now all summer long, wild turkeys had been sneaking out from the woods, eating up seeds I'd planted in the fields. Were those birds bold! First I tried scaring them off by banging pans and practicing my moose call, but they acted stone deaf. "Gobble, gobble," they'd say, and gobble they did.

Then I dredged up a shirt, added my raggedy felt hat, and rigged up a scarecrow, trying to save our crops. But those turkeys weren't scared, not by a chipmunk's chin! Why, they ate up the shirt buttons and carried off my hat. In fact, the next time I saw it, that battered old hat was perched on the Bradford Congregational Church steeple. The Fourth of July, it was, with Major Henley fixing to lead the parade from the Town Hall to Clarence Hobb's blacksmith shop. Actually, Henley wasn't a major, wasn't even a soldier, but he always led the parade because he owned the biggest, fanciest house in Bradford.

Wouldn't you know it, just as the parade began, that hat blew down and landed on Major Henley's skittish mare. Settled right over the horse's eyes. Well, that mare reared up, sliding Major Henley bottom first—*splat*—into the village horse trough, then took off. Blinded by the hat, it galloped through the parade, scattering everyone willy-west, and ran head-hurtle into the Congregational Church door—which wasn't open. Henley's mare never was worth much after that ...nor was the church door! And Major Henley never led the Fourth of July parade again. Believe it or not, that guilty hat flopped off right at my feet, and in all the frappity, nobody noticed me quick scoop it up and stuff it into my pocket.

Well finally, 'long about November, thinking back to how much trouble those turkeys had caused, I decid- ed to go hunting for one. Fattened from eating my seeds, a plump turkey would taste mighty good for Thanksgiving dinner. Besides, a fox had sneaked into the chicken coop one night, and we didn't have any hens left—just some scrawny chicks and a bunch of feathers.

Lulie talked about baking a ham, but I talked turkey for Thanksgiving. Now wild turkeys are smart and hammer-hard to hunt, but they were thick this year and I assured Lulie I could fetch us one. So she searched out a patch of wild cranberries over by the swamp and cooked them into sauce. Then she baked extra cornbread for stuffing, even found wild mushrooms to fancy it up. Along with potatoes, squash, pickles, and pumpkin pie, what a Thanksgiving feast we'd have!

Anyway, the day before Thanksgiving, I set out, gun on shoulder. Pulled on my raggedy felt hat, figuring maybe the turkeys would light on *me*, taking me for that summer scarecrow. Light snow had fallen during the night and tracking a bird would be easy, I was sumac-certain. Yep, right there by the edge of the field, I spotted tracks. Lots of crisscrossed bird tracks in the snow, easy to follow into the woods. In about the time it takes a squirrel to shinny up a beech tree, I came upon a wild turkey skittering along the forest path as much as to say, "Catch me."

For about an hour I followed that bird, which kept just out of my range. Then it stopped and I stopped. Turning its bald head, wattles wobbling, that turkey looked me direct-dodger in the eye. I grabbed up my gun and got all set to "aim-bang-dinner," when I heard a loud "gobble, gobble, gobble" off to my right. There through the trees was another turkey, lots bigger'n the one I had a bead on. So off I tramped after the second bird.

I followed that big turkey over fallen logs and across ice-threaded streams and around barn-sized boulders, right up to the East Branch of Cold River. Then it stopped and I stopped. It stared and I stared. Got my gun up to my shoulder, all ready to pull the trigger, when off to my left, I heard "gobble, gobble, gobble." I looked through the trees and there was *another* turkey—huge, fat, the largest turkey I'd ever seen! Why, it was so enormous, I bet not even Major Henley would have a bird of such amplitude for Thanksgiving dinner.

So of course I set off, chasing after *that* bird. And what a chase it turned out to be! Up one side of Vittum Hill and down t'other, across the West Branch of Cold River on slippery rocks and right up to the edge of Murkell Swamp. But the turkey didn't stop. Not looking east nor slantwise, it went swack into the swamp. I followed, hopping from hillock to hillock, just waiting for that huge bird to slow up so's I could shoot it. Then it stopped and I stopped. That enormous bird turned, glared an eyewink, then spread its wide wings and flapped right at me, wattles waving!

I was so startled, I lost my balance. My gun flew into the air and my left foot plopped into the frigid swamp mud. Busy trying to keep from falling all the way in, I never did see where my gun landed. Anyway, I had to pull and pull and pull to get my foot out of the mire. And all the while, getting fainter and farther away, I could hear "gobble, gobble, gobble"— that wild turkey laughing at me as it disappeared.

Finally I yanked my foot free, but without my boot—lost forever in the depths of Murkell Swamp.

Nothing for it but to pull off my old hat and put it on my foot. Wound it round with my heavy scarf Lulie'd knit, so's my foot wouldn't get frostbit. I hobbled home—gunless, bootless, and turkeyless.

When I finally limped into the house, filthy and empty-handed, Lulie didn't utter a word—'cept when I pulled off my mucky boot. She picked it up and waved it back and forth. She said, "Well, I guess I'll have to find a way to stuff *that* and roast it for Thanksgiving dinner." And we both had to laugh.

Of course, we didn't really roast my boot for Thanksgiving. Nope. But we stuffed ourselves with potatoes, squash, pickles and pumpkin pie. With cranberry sauce and cornbread with wild mushrooms. A mighty delicious dinner even if we didn't have a turkey. Vegetarian, you might say. But we were truly grateful for what we had, believe you me. As Lulie put it:

"Let us give thanks for all we own,
Our family together, our home and hearth.
For all the food we reap from the earth…"
Then she grinned and added,
"And for Thanksgiving turkeys in years to come."

"Didn't that story make you hungry? Why can't we eat yet?" Novia asked. "Where's Papa Alonzo? Why isn't he here?"

She ran to the kitchen window and nearly tripped over Willy. The dog stood by the door, nose pointing, quivering all over like a bowl of cranberry jelly. When Novia pulled the door open for the old dog, Willy dashed out fast as a hummingbird homing in on red beebalm. At the same moment, Papa Alonzo came in with an armload of wood for the stove.

"Come here, everybody—listen!" Novia called and all the Leatherbys crowded around her. "Do you hear it? What is that noise, Papa?"

From across the fields, they could hear "gobble, gobble, gobble." Then farther away, towards Murkell Swamp, they heard, "gobble, gobble, gobble."

"It's those turnip-noodled wild turkeys again," Papa Alonzo said, "Still laughing at us."

Watching the dog race across the fields, Novia clapped her hands. "Papa, do you think maybe Willy'll catch us a turkey?" she asked.

IX.

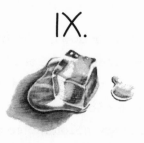

The Tallest Christmas Tree in Carroll County

T he morning before Christmas was cold, so cold that the weather vane on top of the barn froze in place. Instead of shifting with the wind, the iron cock could only face north, shiver, and sneeze three times.

It was so cold that when Fletcher looked out at Polliwog Pond, hoping the ice was thick enough for skating, he saw the whole pond rise up into the air and disappear, heading south! Seems a flock of Canada geese had rested overnight in the pond. Come dawn, their feet'd frozen solid! When they took off, Polliwog Pond went with them like a giant pancake in the sky. Lulie said she sure-as-sherbet hoped that when the geese—and pond—reached Mexico for the winter, the sun'd melt those birds loose. And any polliwogs, too.

In fact, it was so cold that when Papa Alonzo squatted beside his cows and squeezed, instead of milk, he got a pail full of ice cream. When he clumped in from the barn and tried to set down the milk pails, his gloves were tight-frozen to the handles. Lulie had to fetch the crowbar from the back shed to pry him loose so's the younguns could have breakfast.

William worried that he wouldn't like breakfast but once he'd tasted it, he said, "Ice cream on oatmeal is del-*ice*-shus!"

"Sure is cold," Papa complained. "Colder'n a glacier gone west! I swear it's cold enough to freeze the words right out of my mouth. Almost as cold as last winter when all my tales froze in midair."

Lulie laughed. "You need to tell some new ones. By now, all your tales are twice-told, tattered, and scattered to the winds. The pantry's bare!"

Papa Alonzo peered out the window. "I may indeed have a new tale to tell before *this* day's done! That sky looks lowering enough to scrape its belly on Ragged Mountain and spill out prodigious piles of snow. Producing a whiter Christmas than we want!"

Then he sighed. "However, I sure-as-sliding hope we don't get snow till night. I'm riding Macduff over to Miz Millicent Campbell's with a cow in tow. Pore Miz Campbell's plumb out of milk and her with three sets of twins! Tansy's our best milker, but we can loan her a spell." He paused. "Hope that moose won't appear before I leave."

You see, way back in early October, an enormous bull moose had shown up at the north pasture one morning. Maybe he hadn't found a cow moose to love during mating season. Maybe he just fancied the Leatherbys' little yellow cow, although Tansy never so

much as "mooed" in answer to the moose's amorous
looks. Day after day he waited, leaning against the
north pasture gate. Each evening when the cows
were herded into the barn to be milked, the moose
bellowed like a bassoon with a bellyache and slunk
into the woods. Come dawn, when the cows returned
to the pasture, there he'd be, making moose eyes at
Tansy.

Now Papa Alonzo wasn't exactly afraid of that
moose, no siree-sugarplums, even though the animal
was so tall he could look eye-to-eye with the hayloft
mice. But a bull moose in love? Not a creature to cross
horns and pitchfork handles with! Whenever Lulie'd
ask, "How about chasing away that moose?" Papa'd
just shrug and say "Love's stronger than sassafras."
Whatever that meant.

Anyway, imagine! Here it was, the day before
Christmas and Papa Alonzo fixing to leave. April
grabbed his sleeve, tears leaking down her cheeks.
"But Papa," she sniffled, "What about our Christmas
tree? You promised we'd look for one this afternoon."

"Oh, don't you worry a partridge berry! I'll be
home in good time to go chop us a tree before dark —
the tallest ever," he said.

Papa Alonzo looked all around outside — no
moose. So he quick saddled up Macduff while Lulie
bundled an old quilt over Tansy so's her milk wouldn't
freeze solid. Then he climbed up and clucked to
Macduff, eager to be off. Waving goodbye, he called
back, "You younguns make bushel basketsful of deco-

rations! I promise, this year the Leatherbys are going to have the tallest tree in Carroll County!"

So that's how the nine children spent the morning—stringing popcorn and dried berries, cutting and pasting, painting pine cones—busier than six squirrels in a beechnut tree. When they finished, they ran to the kitchen window to watch for Papa Alonzo's return. "Oh, look!" they all moaned.

Rain was falling, a heavy drizzle. Not snow, but rain. And with the temperature way below freezing, it was turning to ice faster than cream churns to butter. Lilacs and birches bowed and shivered under a cape of ice. Pines stood like silver arrows aimed into the gray sky.

Willy was whining outside. When Lulie opened the door, he sneezed, and a shower of sleet rattled against the door. But his paws were stuck fast to the ice! Lulie had to run lickety-limbo for the teakettle to melt that dog off the doorstep. Once inside, Willy bellied down under the warm stove and wouldn't come out, not even when baby Moses offered him a ham bone.

About midafternoon, the younger Leatherbys began to whimper while the older ones began to whisper. How would Papa get home? Miz Millicent Campbell's house was way down Three Horse Hill in Strump Hollow. With the road ice-coated, Papa'd never, ever get back up steep Three Horse Hill. And even if Papa did return before nightfall, how could they find the tallest tree in Carroll County and drag it back when the whole world was one shiny ocean of ice? Every now and then a child would say, with a voice as sad as yesterday's potato peels, "No Christmas tree this year."

Blump, blump, bang! It was the wee hours of the morning, nearly sun up. All the Leatherbys had fallen asleep hours ago, but the loud noise awakened them. Papa Alonzo?! Lulie lit the lamp and nine yawning younguns crowded into the kitchen. Papa stomped into the room. "I am exhausticated!" he muttered, "as tired as a turned-over turtle."

"How'd you get home from Strump Hollow? With all the ice! Was it slippery-slick?" Everyone talked at once.

Papa Alonzo yawned, but looking at the circle of eager faces, he said, "Well, to tell the truth, once I'd delivered Tansy, I did pause a wagon's worth, wondering how Macduff would navigate the ice up Three Horse Hill. But I worry-wagered about finding our Christmas tree, too. So about midafternoon I decided to start for home. Down in Strump Hollow we skidded sidewinders, but it was Three Horse Hill that stymied us. Every time Macduff plodded up two feet, we slid back three. Got so's I was afraid we'd slide right back beyond last Saturday!

"When we skimmed past her door for about the tenth time, trying to make a run for it, Miz Millicent Campbell pulled us in. By then it was supper time, so she fed us—oats for Macduff, boiled beef with horse-radish sauce for me. Miz Campbell commenced telling how she'd reaped a humongous harvest of horseradish last fall—bushels and barrels stored in the root cellar. That gave me an idea! Now, you all know how hot horseradish is, how it tickles your nose and makes your eyes teary. Right?" He looked around.

"Well, I stuffed a burlap sack with horseradish roots and fed some to Macduff. Whoosh! That horse took off like a shooting star with me clinging to the reins for dear dumplings! What with his nostrils breathing fire and his eyes streaming hot tears, Macduff melted us a path all the way home. Didn't need a lantern to see by, neither! Course I had to lean over constantly and stuff horseradish into his mouth to stoke the fire. My right arm feels about six inches longer than it was! Besides which, I suspect my jacket sleeve is scorched beyond mending. To say nothing of Macduff's singed reins."

Papa Alonzo's face was sad. He said, "Younguns, I'm sorry about that Christmas tree. Come sunup, maybe the ice'll melt a mite and we can walk into the woods. Find us a tree, even though it's already Christmas Day."

Nine Leatherbys began to wriggle and giggle. Even Lulie laughed. But chatterbox Martha spoke first. "Wait a widgeon, Papa Alonzo!" She opened the door and reached out. In a bear's breath she was back, carrying a berry basket filled with chunks of ice.

As you know, Martha wanted more than anything

in the world to be a storyteller like Papa Alonzo. And she'd decided that the Leatherbys' Christmas Eve was indeed a good story! Just before she went to bed, she'd stuck her head out the door and begun to talk — wanted to practice her tale. It was so cold that her words froze in midair — just like Papa Alonzo's tales last year! That gave Martha an idea. She'd grabbed her frozen words and popped them into a basket. For safekeeping.

Papa looked mighty puzzled, so Martha marched over to the stove, lifted the lid of the teakettle and dumped in the basketful. Out of the spout of the teakettle, her words began to pour, a little misty from all that steam. Baby Moses climbed onto her lap and all the Leatherbys gathered close as Martha's tale began.

W ell, now, as I recollect…we worried and waited all afternoon for you, Papa Alonzo, running to the window so often we wore a two-foot furrow in the floorboards — deep enough to plant parsnips! Along about five o'clock, we heard a crash in the parlor, a thud, and then a loud mournful bellow. "Tansy's moose!" we all shouted, and ran into the room. Sure enough, there, his head poking through the window like one of Major Henley's hunting trophies, was the bull moose. Slap dab where we always put our Christmas tree.

What a sight for Christmas Eve! No tree, no

Papa, only Tansy's moose, moping, his antlers tickling the ceiling and taking up half the parlor. How he ever got that enormous spread of antlers through the window was a mystery! The beast's huge head and shoulders were wedged against the window frame so tightly that we didn't feel the outside cold. Mama Lulie called out, "Shoo! Scat!" but whoever saw a moose "Shoo" or "Scat"?

Besides, that big old moose looked so lonely and so unhappy, none of us had the heart to scare him away. We hoped maybe he'd move on in a minute. But that moose didn't move a muscle. Just kept looking at us as if to say, "Where's my Tansy?" As it turned out, the moose couldn't have moved even if he'd wanted. In less than the time Reverend Wigglesworth would need to recite the Thirty-third Psalm from his pulpit—backwards—the animal's hooves were stuck in ice so thick, it'd take seven sunny Saturdays to melt.

At first, we were a bit wary-watchful. That animal was so huge! But then baby Moses toddled right up, patted the moose's chin and said, "Nice doggie." We all stopped breathing for the flicker of a fire ember but the bull moose just sighed and his mouth turned up in a midgety morsel of a smile.

The minutes ticked by, with the parlor clock's Bing-Bong announcing five, five-thirty, six—supper time! We gathered around Mama in the kitchen, helping her dish up Jacob's Cattle beans and sausages. Then we heard a strange sound echo through the house. A sound like a cross between a runaway rail-

road engine and a coyote with a sore throat. That
moose! Was he whimpering because he was lonely for
Tansy? Or because he had cold feet? Or....

Well, the twins pulled Mama down to whisper in
each ear—"He's hungry!" So Mama Lulie filled her
dishpan with beans and sausages. Jemma took one
side, Jethro the other, and into the parlor they
marched. You know, that moose stopped whining and
quick as a chickadee quit being a vegetarian. He gobbled up the food, burped once, then shook his antlers
to dislodge a skinny sausage hanging there.

That was funny! We laughed even harder when
baby Moses toddled over, trailing a string of cranberries. Moses said, "Kiss moose," and kissed the animal
smack on his big nose.

Without a word, we all ran to get *our* Christmas
tree decorations. Of course, we had to climb on chairs
and stretch high to reach, but before long, the moose's
antlers had nearly disappeared under strings of popcorn and garlands of fruit. I boosted baby Moses up
so's he could hang a gingerbread figure and shiny pine
cone on every prong. The moose just kept grinning
and breathing contented-sounding sighs, making the
gingerbread figures dance. For the final touch, I found
our long belt of sleigh bells and looped them around
the moose's antlers.

Octava said, "Oh, look at our tree—I bet it *is* the
tallest in Carroll County!"

"Well, if not the tallest, it sure is the *most unusual*
Christmas tree in Carroll County!" April added.

William laughed and said, "You mean Chrismoose tree!"

So we all joined hands and danced in a circle, singing our favorite song. "Oh, Chrismoose tree, oh, Chrismoose tree!" Three verses. The moose joined in, humming and jiggling his head, jingling the sleigh bells right in rhythm with our song. The tune was clear as a bell. Believe it or not!

M artha's last words had thawed just as the teakettle ran out of steam. Papa Alonzo said proudly, "Martha, I do believe you are going to be the best storyteller in Carroll County!"

"Thank you, Papa," she said, blushing, then added, "Papa, we were certain you'd not get home until morning, so a little before midnight we wished each other—and our moose tree—a Merry Christmas and all of us went to sleep."

Four-year-old Novia giggled. "All except me," she said. "Papa, I stayed awake until midnight all by myself. Remember? You told us that when the clock strikes twelve on Christmas Eve, animals can talk!"

"Huh, I bet that moose didn't say anything," Fletcher said, making a face.

Novia nodded. "He did! He said, 'Well, now as I recollect...' but then I...then I fell asleep and...."

A loud fla-lump and jingle from the parlor inter-rupted her. All the Leatherbys rushed to the door and pushed it open. "Oh, no!" The room was empty. They ran to the open window. In the pale sunrise glow of Christmas morning, they could see the moose hurrying off, strings of popcorn streaming from his antlers.

"Going home, I imagine," Lulie said. "Back to the woods."

"No—look!" Papa Alonzo pointed. "That moose is heading down the road toward Strump Hollow. Must be he wants to find Tansy and wish *her* a Merry Christmas!"

"Kiss moose," baby Moses said, waving.

"Listen!" Martha exclaimed.

As the moose ran, sleigh bells rang out, playing the tune loud and clear, "Oh, Chrismoose tree, oh Chrismoose tree…"

From way down in Strump Hollow, a faint sound echoed through the air. "Moo, moo, moose…."

But that's another story.